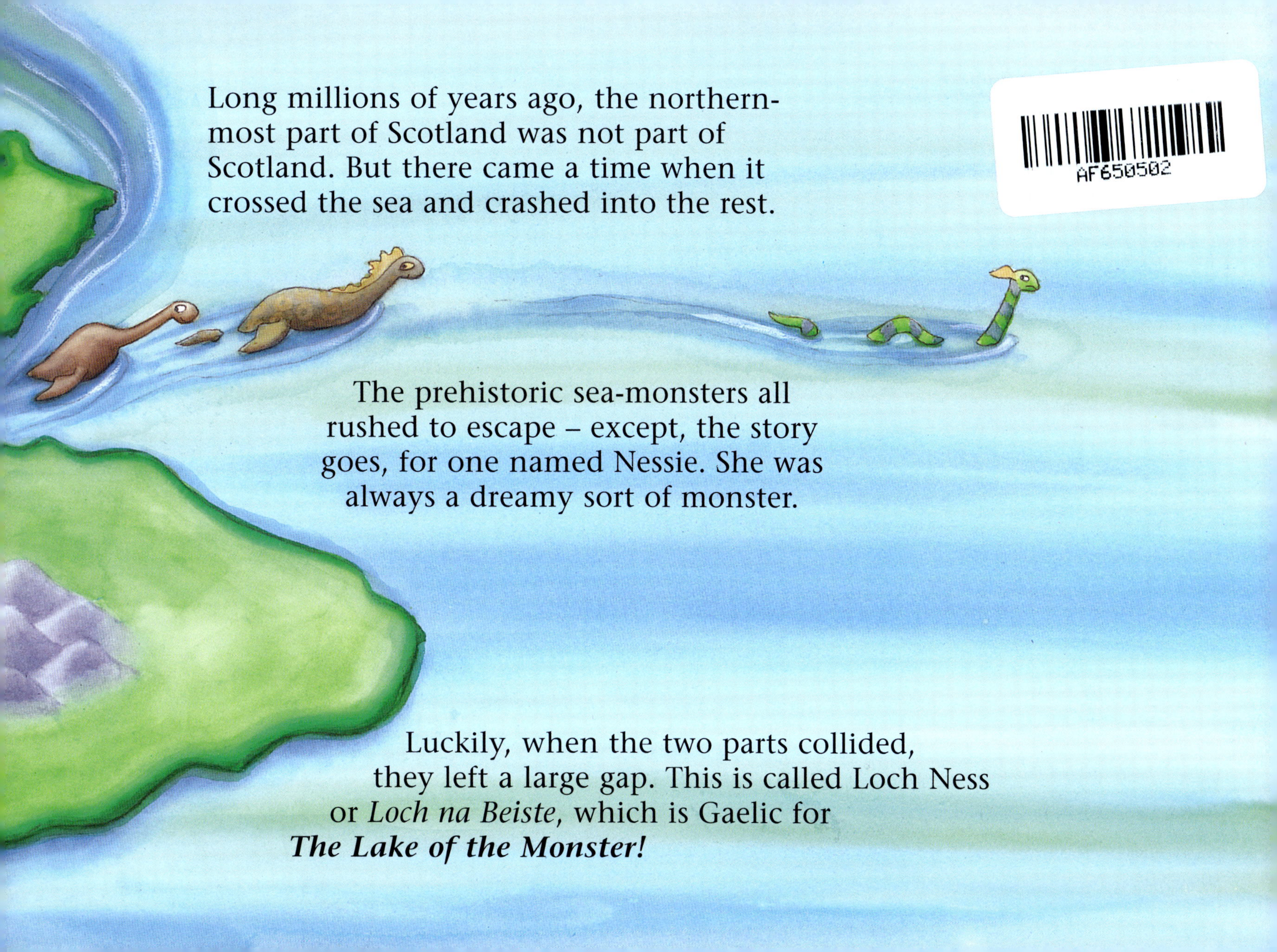

Long millions of years ago, the northern-most part of Scotland was not part of Scotland. But there came a time when it crossed the sea and crashed into the rest.

The prehistoric sea-monsters all rushed to escape – except, the story goes, for one named Nessie. She was always a dreamy sort of monster.

Luckily, when the two parts collided, they left a large gap. This is called Loch Ness or *Loch na Beiste*, which is Gaelic for ***The Lake of the Monster!***

Loch Ness is so deep that you could stand three Big Bens in it and they would still not reach the top.

The Statue of Liberty could dive in happily without any chance of her head hitting the bottom.

NESSIE THE LOCH NESS MONSTER

Richard Brassey

Orion
Children's Books

In memory of my father

First published in Great Britain in 1996 by Orion Children's Books
Reissued in 2010 by Orion Children's Books
This edition published in 2016 by Hodder and Stoughton Limited

21

A CIP catalogue record for this book is available from the British Library.

ISBN 978 1 4440 0056 6

Printed in China

FSC www.fsc.org MIX Paper from responsible sources FSC® C104740

Orion Children's Books
An imprint of
Hachette Children's Group
Part of Hodder & Stoughton Limited
Carmelite House
50 Victoria Embankment
London EC4Y 0DZ

An Hachette UK Company
www.hachette.co.uk

www.hachettechildrens.co.uk

And five jumbo jets could be placed wingtip to wingtip and still have room to loop the loop...

...plenty of room for a monster!

Here Nessie lived happily for a few million years until 565 AD when a man called St Columba, who was busy converting the Scots to Christianity, shouted **"Get back!"** from the bank.

Nessie was surprised but paid no attention.

And, for a thousand years or more, she was left in peace to swim to and fro in the loch. Occasionally she would also stroll amongst the hills.

The monks of St Benedict's Abbey kept a careful record of sightings.

The beautiful Urquhart Castle was built beside the loch, but the people who lived there were far too busy fighting off attackers to have any time for monsters.

Eventually they left and the castle fell into ruins.

But then in 1933 disaster struck.

A road was built along the edge of the loch.
The noise was frightful, what with crashing and banging and rocks splashing into the water all day long.

After that came the traffic, bumper to bumper. What was a monster to do?

Everywhere Nessie went there were people.

She tried to keep out of their way, but one day, while sneaking over the road for a wee wander in the heather, she was spotted by Mr and Mrs George Spicer from London, England.

And that was the end of Nessie's peaceful time. Newspapers all over the world were full of the story. A famous circus ringmaster offered £100,000 to anybody who could catch the monster for him.

People poured into the Scottish Highlands. The new road beside the loch became even more crowded. Everybody claimed to have seen the monster!

Some of them said it had a head like a sheep. Others described a shaggy mane. Most thought it had a long neck, but did it have a tail? Was it as big as a house or only the size of a cow?

A few brave souls came within a hair's breadth of catching it.

One of the newspapers sent a big game hunter to track Nessie.

The hunter thought it would be more fun to make his own monster tracks with a stuffed hippo leg which he used as an umbrella stand.

Everybody was fooled. Photos of *Monster Footprints* were in all the papers.

One day a surgeon who was driving by the loch was startled to see Nessie. He took a photo.

It did not come out very clearly. Perhaps his hands were shaking at the time. But it is still the best photo of Nessie that anyone has yet taken.

Whether the surgeon's hands were still shaking when he later removed an appendix in Inverness is not known.

Everybody wanted to find out how Nessie came to be in Loch Ness and why she looked different to each person who saw her. Some people said that she came and went through mysterious tunnels connecting Loch Ness to the sea. They said there were other monsters too.

They couldn't explain why the water in the loch didn't run away through the tunnels.

Other people said that Nessie was simply the proud mother of a whole family of wee monsters ... though who the father was they did not care to say.

One day two boys out fishing noticed three very queer little creatures swimming behind their boat.

They told the monks of St Benedict's, who knew at once what they had really seen – **baby monsters!**

A great expedition was organised. Twenty men watched the loch for a whole month and one of them actually filmed the monster.

The film was rushed to London and shown to some famous zoologists. The zoologists pretended to know what Nessie was, though they hadn't a clue.

The film was never seen again.

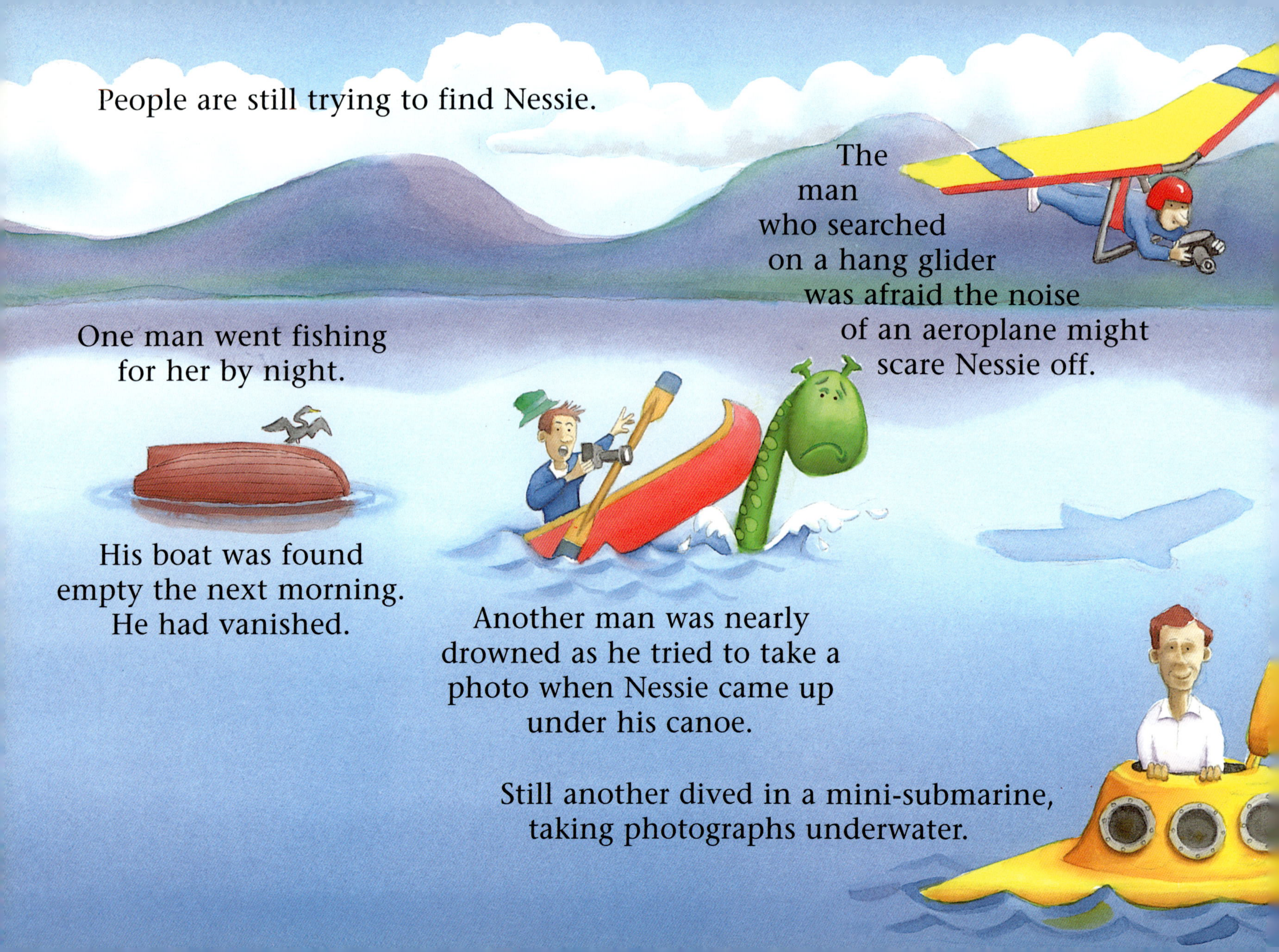

People are still trying to find Nessie.

One man went fishing for her by night.

His boat was found empty the next morning. He had vanished.

Another man was nearly drowned as he tried to take a photo when Nessie came up under his canoe.

The man who searched on a hang glider was afraid the noise of an aeroplane might scare Nessie off.

Still another dived in a mini-submarine, taking photographs underwater.

Some people would like to drain the loch so they can search the bottom. Others devise complicated traps which never seem to work.

A group of scientists tried boats fitted with sonar, which is what bats use to find insects.

And there's one man who has searched up and down the loch for thirty years or more. He did once catch a glimpse of Nessie.

But nobody has ever got close enough to Nessie to capture her.

Could it be that over the years she has grown to rather enjoy the game of hide and seek?